Elephant Park

Written by
Melanie Koster

Illustrated by
Jenny Cooper

SCHOLASTIC
SYDNEY AUCKLAND NEW YORK TORONTO LONDON MEXICO CITY
NEW DELHI HONG KONG BUENOS AIRES PUERTO RICO

For Mum and Bee,
who believe in the magic of stories ~ MK

For Poppy ~ JC

This story is inspired by the iconic elephant slide in Bishopdale Park in Ōtautahi Christchurch, affectionately referred to as 'The Elephant Park' by locals. Built in the 1970s, the elephant slide has brought joy to generations and the park has become a popular meeting place for families from all walks of life.

“Are you okay?” Noah asked the old grey elephant.

The elephant twitched an ear and sighed. Her tusks were chipped, her trunk was cracked and the paint was flaking off her toenails.

“I’m tired,” said the elephant.

Noah climbed up and rubbed behind the elephant's ear. "Why are you tired?"

"I've been standing in this park for a very long time."

"How long?" Noah asked.

"Well . . . I remember your father playing here when he was about your age," said the elephant.

"That was a long time ago," said Noah. "And a long time to stand in one spot. Have you never been anywhere else?"

"No. I couldn't. You children need me here."

The boy looked around.

“There aren’t many children playing on you today.”

The elephant sighed. “No . . . now they have the flying fox, the swings and the fancy new mega-slide. Sometimes the bigger kids skateboard down me. It was exciting when I was younger, but I must admit that, now I'm old, it gives me a headache.”

“I think you need a holiday,” said Noah. “Why don't you come home with me for the rest of the weekend?”

“That’s very kind of you,” said the elephant. She groaned and her bones clicked and creaked as she stretched her stiff legs. She slipped out from under the ladder onto the cool grass.

It wasn’t far to Noah’s house, which was just as well.

“Hello, old friend,” Dad said to the elephant. “You look very tired indeed. What you need is a nice cup of tea and a lie down.”

Dad helped Noah make a space for the elephant to rest. The old grey elephant lay in the shade of the pear tree and went to sleep.

At dinnertime, Noah foraged in the vegetable garden and fetched the elephant a bucket of carrots, potatoes and bok choy. Dad brought out mint chip ice cream and strawberries for dessert.

Noah filled up the paddling pool
with water and they all cooled off.

The elephant squeezed through the patio doors into the lounge and they watched movies late into the night. Dad made popcorn with extra butter.

Noah's bottom bunk was a bit of a squash for the elephant, so they decided to camp out in the back yard.

Noah read jokes from his library book and the elephant sang until they felt sleepy.

In the morning, Dad cooked pancakes with golden syrup for breakfast. He made an N-shaped one for Noah and an E-shape for the elephant.

The elephant said it was the nicest breakfast she'd had in a very long time.

Dad found a photograph of himself as a little boy, playing at Elephant Park.

"Look," said Noah to the elephant, "your tusks weren't broken then. There are no cracks in your trunk either."

The elephant sighed. "See how polished and perfect my toenails were."

"Hmmmm, I wonder . . ." said Dad. "Would you like a makeover?"

Dad led the elephant to the garage and heaved the toolbox from his work van. He filled the elephant's gaps and fixed her broken tusks. He shaped and smoothed and sanded.

Noah carefully hand-painted the elephant's toenails until they gleamed like china dinner plates.

"Ooh! It tickles!" laughed the elephant
as Dad gave her a respray in glimmering grey.

"I feel like a young calf again!"

laughed the elephant, and she spun around, admiring her reflection in the window.

When it was time to leave, the elephant helped Noah and his father climb up onto her back. As they headed down Oaktree Lane, people hurried out of their homes.

"Dear old Elly!" Mrs Henderson exclaimed. "I remember sliding down your back with my sisters," she said. "Do you remember me?"

The elephant smiled. "An elephant never forgets," she said. "You had your sixth birthday party at my park."

“I knocked a tooth out when I fell off your ladder,” said Mr Sisifa.

The elephant winked. “You were very brave.”

“Are you going back home now?” a little girl asked.

“If you’ll come and visit me,” said the elephant.

The crowd grew and they all joined in the procession back to Elephant Park. Mr Sisifa raced home to whip up an elephantine batch of scones with cream and homemade plum jam.

Everyone spread out picnic blankets and Mrs Henderson passed around lemonade and sliced watermelon.

They played tag, hide and seek, and all of them had a turn on the elephant slide.

Are you okay now?" Noah asked the elephant.

"I'm still tired," said the elephant. "But it's a good kind of tired. Thank you for being my friend."

“Will you be here tomorrow after school?” said Noah.

“I’ll be here,” said the elephant.

“See you tomorrow!” Noah called.

The elephant slipped back under the ladder,
raised her trunk and let out a long, loud trumpet.